Elspeth Hart
and the
Magnificent Rescue

Pedro, this one's for you – SF
For the magnificent Amélie – JB

STRIPES PUBLISHING
An imprint of Little Tiger Press
1 The Coda Centre, 189 Munster Road,
London SW6 6AW

A paperback original
First published in Great Britain in 2016

ISBN: 978-1-84715-667-9

Printed and bound in the UK.

10 9 8 7 6 5 4 3 2 1

Elspeth Hart
and the
Magnificent Rescue

Sarah Forbes

Illustrated by James Brown

1
The Very Fancy Private Plane

It was the middle of the night and Elspeth Hart was in a tiny plane high above the Australian coast. She was peering out of the window at the darkness below, feeling very small and very far from home.

Until she was ten years old, Elspeth Hart had led a pretty normal life, living in a quiet village with her mum and dad, who owned a sweet shop. Elspeth was small for her age, and a little bit shy, and her favourite colour was purple. In fact, the only thing you might notice about Elspeth Hart was her hair, which was dark and wild and hard to control. But last year, Elspeth's world had turned upside down, and now NOTHING was normal any more.

Elspeth had been kidnapped by two awful women called Miss Crabb and Gladys Goulash. Those nasty ladies were trying

Miss Crabb

to get hold of something very special: Elspeth's top-secret family recipe for sticky

Gladys Goulash

toffee sauce. They knew that if they had the recipe, they could make loads of money selling the sauce.

6

Miss Crabb and Gladys Goulash worked as dinner ladies in a dreadful boarding school full of show-off pupils, and Elspeth had been trapped there for a whole year. Elspeth shivered as she remembered it. But she had made one friend in the school: Rory Snitter, who was sitting across from Elspeth on the plane, snoring gently.

Rory Snitter

Elspeth looked over at Rory and remembered how he'd helped her escape from the school, and how Miss Crabb and Gladys Goulash had come after her, stolen her secret family recipe, and sneaked off to New York on a giant cruise ship called the *HMS Unsinkable.* Elspeth and Rory had chased them on to the ship and had the adventure of their lives getting the precious recipe back.

Now the recipe was tucked safely inside Elspeth's trainer … and Elspeth was on another very important mission. She knew that Miss Crabb had tricked her parents into going to Australia to look for her. And Elspeth was determined to find her mum and dad. I'm sure you can imagine, dear reader, that if someone you loved had been tricked into going all the way to Australia to look for you, you would want to go and find them straight away.

Elspeth and Rory weren't in a normal plane, like the ones you might travel in to go on holiday. They were in Rory's parents' private plane, and Rory's butler, Mr Tunnock, was flying it. Mr Tunnock was a marvellous butler. He was very sensible, very responsible, and had very good contacts with other butlers all over the world through the International

Butler Network. He knew how to drive a car and ride a unicycle and sail a sailing boat and, best of all, he had a pilot's licence.

Across the aisle, Rory stirred and rubbed his eyes. "Can you see anything out there?" he asked, sitting up. He reached into his pocket and unwrapped a chocolate for his pet lizard, Lazlo.

Lazlo grabbed the chocolate with his tiny claws and started nibbling it.

"Not a thing. It's still too dark," Elspeth said, taking the chocolate Rory was offering her. "But we can't be far away." She wriggled around in her seat, trying to get comfortable.

Rory's mum had had the plane decorated in shades of pink and purple, with fake diamonds everywhere. It looked very fancy, but the sparkly seats weren't comfy to sit on.

"I wonder what Mr Collins will be like,"
Rory said, eating another chocolate. Mr
Collins was a butler friend of Mr Tunnock,
who had promised to meet them as soon as
they landed in Australia. "Perhaps he'll be
just like Tunnock."

Mr Tunnock hardly ever spoke. He liked

everything to be neat and tidy, and he didn't do anything without making a plan first.

It hadn't been easy to get Mr Tunnock to fly Rory's parents' private jet all the way to Australia. He had said it was dangerous and foolish and he had better take Elspeth and Rory home at once. But Rory said he wasn't going anywhere without Elspeth, and then Mr Tunnock said he wasn't going anywhere without Rory. Rory was hoping his parents would never find out they'd borrowed the plane, because they were away on a super-luxurious holiday for three months.

Elspeth fiddled with the wrapper from her chocolate. It was bright gold and it reminded her of the sweet wrappers from her parents' shop. She had a sudden vivid memory of standing on a stool when she was little, helping to stir a batch of fudge.

She could picture her mum's smiling face and her dad in his big apron, hunting around for his glasses. Her dad was always losing things.

Elspeth put the wrapper down. "Oh, Rory," she said. "I'm scared. I mean, anything could have happened to my parents! Australia's a huge place. How on earth will I find them?" She blinked hard to stop tears from rolling down her cheeks.

Rory grabbed her hand. "Come on, Elspeth," he said. "Think how brave you've been, escaping from the School for Show-offs and going all the way to America on that big ship. I'm sure you'll find your parents!"

Elspeth took a big, deep breath and nodded. "I just hope Miss Crabb and Gladys Goulash aren't going to come after us again," she said.

Elspeth was almost certain she had seen Miss Crabb and Gladys Goulash rowing away in a lifeboat back in New York. The idea of them following her made Elspeth feel a bit sick.

"Even if they escaped in that lifeboat, they'll be lying low somewhere," Rory said. "They won't risk getting caught again. I'm sure that's the last we'll see of them."

2

Crabb and Goulash
on the Loose

Unfortunately for Elspeth, Miss Crabb
and Gladys Goulash were on their way to
Australia, too. They had hidden in a cargo
plane flying to Sydney, where they'd had a
very squashed and uncomfortable journey,
because they were sitting among huge
crates of ouga ouga fruit.

If you haven't heard of the ouga ouga fruit,

dear reader, it is the smelliest fruit in the world. It smells like a pot of yoghurt that has been sitting on top of a radiator for months.

When the plane landed, Miss Crabb and Gladys Goulash had climbed into an ouga ouga fruit crate, and now they were in a stinky ship travelling around the coast of Australia, heading to a town called Port Bongo.

Gladys Goulash liked the smell of the ouga ouga fruit. In fact, Gladys Goulash had eaten fifteen of them already and was now wondering what to have for pudding. She was trying to get her foot in her mouth so she could chew her own toenails.

"How long are we going to be on this boat?" she asked in a moany voice.

It was pretty dark in the ouga ouga fruit crate, but Miss Crabb gave Gladys Goulash a frosty look anyway.

"Ages," she said. "But it'll be worth it, because we're going to catch that little creep Elspeth Hart once and for all. And we're going to get that secret recipe off her! We can't let her win!"

Gladys burped. "How do you even know Elspeth is going to Australia?" she asked.

"It's obvious," said Miss Crabb scornfully. "You *told* her that her parents were in Australia, you fool! She's desperate to find them. Where else would she go?"

"But how do *we* know her parents will be in Australia?" Gladys asked, scratching her head.

"Nincompoop!" hissed Miss Crabb. "We know her stupid parents will be in Australia, in the Never-ending Rainforest, because I phoned them a couple of weeks ago and told them Elspeth was there, remember? They'll have gone looking for her! I wanted to get them out of the way. But thanks to you and your big mouth, Elspeth knows they're in Australia!"

"I see…" said Gladys Goulash, who didn't really see at all. "Ooh, I'm so hungry. Maybe I could eat this box we're in." She tried to gnaw the side of the crate.

Miss Crabb ignored her sidekick and closed her eyes. "That stupid little snot rag thinks she's so clever," she muttered.

"She thinks she can find her parents and everything will be fine, but we'll be in Australia long before her. Ha!"

"What we gonna do when we arrive, then?" asked Gladys Goulash. She shoved a finger up her nose, looking for a tasty bogey, but she had eaten them all already.

"We're going undercover," said Miss Crabb. "We'll nick one of those takeaway vans! Then we'll drive to Starry Bay, the nearest town to the Never-ending Rainforest." She twisted around, grabbed her grimy rucksack and took out a book called *101 Horrible Punishments*. She peered at it in the gloom with a smirk on her lips.

"I've got a wonderful plan for trapping Elspeth and her soppy parents so we can get that recipe back," she said. "A plan involving spiders and a very big pit! Eee-hee-hee!

Elspeth will track her parents to Starry Bay soon enough. I know how that little creep operates. We just have to get there first and lie low until she arrives."

She opened her greasy notebook and Gladys Goulash screwed up her eyes to read what was inside:

- Follow stupid Elspeth into the rainforest when she goes looking for her parents
- Sneak ahead of her and dig a HUGE pit filled with Australian Bitey Bitey spiders
- Elspeth falls into the pit and can't get out
- I promise to let her go if she gives me the recipe
- I get recipe and then scarper, but ...
- I leave her stuck in the pit to perish! Eee-hee-hee!

Gladys read the plan very slowly. Then she looked up with a confused expression.

"Where you gonna get all them Bitey Bitey spiders from?" she asked.

"I've thought ahead, Gladys Goulash," Miss Crabb said in a smug voice. "There's a shop in Port Bongo, where this ship docks. The nastiest, scariest pet shop anyone could imagine. We'll go on a nice little shopping trip before we head to Starry Bay."

3

The First Proper Clue

It was just getting light as Mr Tunnock landed the tiny Snitter jet on a private airfield near Cairns.

"Gosh," Mr Tunnock said. "I feel dreadfully light-headed in this heat!"

Mr Tunnock was usually very neat and tidy-looking, but after flying all the way from America, he looked ruffled and hot.

Elspeth and Rory helped him down the steps of the little plane, and Elspeth realized her whole body felt heavy with tiredness.

Mr Collins was waiting for them on the tarmac. He wore a smart suit just like Mr Tunnock, but he was very suntanned, and his arms were so muscly they seemed like they were about to pop out of his jacket. He looked tough, but he had a friendly smile.

"Mr Tunnock!" he said as they got off the plane. "G'day! And this must be Elspeth and Rory."

Mr Tunnock wiped a bead of sweat from his forehead and gave a low bow.

"We are terribly grateful for your assistance," he said, straightening his cuffs.

"Ah, no worries!" said Mr Collins. "Anything for a member of the International Butler Network! I'll take you to the hotel I work in. You can have some food and we'll talk. Follow me, mate."

Mr Collins began striding towards a shiny Jeep parked at the side of the airfield.

"Have there been any sightings of my parents?" Elspeth asked, trotting along to keep up. "Anything at all?"

Mr Collins jumped into the Jeep and started the engine. "Possibly," he said. "But we'll need your help, missy."

An hour later, they were all at the Cairns Bonzer Towers Hotel, sitting around a huge shiny table. Mr Tunnock looked much happier after a chance to change his shirt and slick down his hair, but Elspeth was practically hopping from one foot to the other, desperate to know what Mr Collins knew.

"So," Mr Collins said, putting aside his cup of tea and unrolling a big map. "I've been in touch with some other butlers, and some mates who work in hotels and train stations and the like. Now I can't promise anything, but we've had a sighting of a couple matching your parents' description here, then here and here." He jabbed his finger at three different points on the map. "All in the last couple of weeks."

Elspeth felt a wave of excitement. This was *very* good news. She examined the map.

"It looks like they're going further north with each sighting," she said. "I wonder where they're heading."

"Well, let's be sure we've spotted the right people first. We've got a CCTV image to look at," Mr Collins said, opening up a laptop. "A mate up in Boggyville train station thought he'd seen a pair that sounded like your parents last week. Take a look…"

Elspeth leaned towards the computer screen. She looked at the images carefully, her heart hammering. The pictures showed a quiet train station, and every so often figures would move across the screen as people arrived and left. But when Mr Collins stopped the clip, there they were: her mum and dad. There was her mum's curly dark hair and her dad's battered old green rucksack.

"Yes, that's them! I'm almost certain," she said. "Can you zoom in, Mr Collins?"

Mr Collins did, and the picture got a bit blurry, but Elspeth could see that it was definitely her parents. "Yes!" she said. "That's Mum and Dad!" She reached out a hand and gently touched the screen.

"Oh wow, Elspeth," Rory said. "Your parents *are* in Australia!"

Elspeth screwed up her eyes to see better. "It looks like Dad is sticking something on the wall there," she said slowly. "Mr Collins, can you get a clearer picture so we can see what it is?"

Mr Collins furrowed his brow. "I'm not sure I know how to do that, mate," he said, but Rory was at his side in a flash.

"Let me try," he said.

Rory sat down at the laptop and made a few adjustments. He frowned and chewed his lip and for a few minutes the room was completely silent.

"Hmm, it's a bit tricky," Rory said. He tapped at the keyboard and clicked a couple more times, screwing up his nose in frustration. Elspeth held her breath.

All of a sudden, Rory's eyes lit up.

"Got it!" he said. "Look!"

Elspeth leaned in. The image was perfectly clear.

MISSING

Have you seen our daughter?

Our precious daughter Elspeth Hart was kidnapped in the UK over a year ago. We are in Australia trying to find her. We had a tip-off that she might be in the Never-ending Rainforest, but we will follow up any leads. We are desperate to bring her home.

There is a reward of $1,000 for any information leading us to our daughter.

Please phone 04888 183 302 if you can help.

"Rory, you're a genius!" Elspeth cried. "Our first proper clue!"

Elspeth leaped up and ran to the phone in the corner of the room. She dialled the number from the poster with shaking hands. It started to ring.

4
The Road North

The phone rang and rang. Elspeth felt so full of excitement, she didn't think she'd be able to speak. Who would pick up, her mum or her dad? At the thought of hearing their voices, her heart swelled up like a balloon.

But the phone rang for a long time with no answer. Finally there were three beeps and the line went dead. Elspeth hung up and dialled the number again, but the same thing happened.

"It's a dead end," she said sadly, putting down the phone. "The number isn't working."

"I'm sorry, Elspeth," Rory said sympathetically.

Elspeth sat down again and pulled the big map towards her. She'd just have to find another way. "The poster mentioned the Never-ending Rainforest," she murmured, tracing her finger across the map. "There it is. The nearest town is Starry Bay. That's where we need to go!"

Mr Collins looked very serious. "There are rumours it's haunted, that rainforest. Folk have heard very strange noises there, especially at night."

"Oh, but we have to go!" Elspeth said, jumping up and grabbing her bag. "We can't hang about. If Mum and Dad think I'm in that rainforest, they will have gone in looking for me. What's the fastest way to get there?"

"Driving, mate," said Mr Colllins. "No trains beyond Boggyville, and no airfield for a plane. You know what ... take my Jeep." He threw a set of keys towards Mr Tunnock, who tried to grab them and missed.

"Terribly kind of you," Mr Tunnock said, scrabbling around for the keys on the floor. "We shall of course return your vehicle as soon as our ... expedition ... is over."

Hours later, they still hadn't reached Starry Bay. They were driving north as fast as Mr Tunnock was willing to drive, which wasn't very fast at all. Mr Tunnock refused to break the speed limit, and Elspeth wished she was old enough to take the wheel so she could get them to Starry Bay faster. Instead, she was sitting in the passenger seat next to Mr Tunnock with a map, working out the route.

It felt to Elspeth as if they had been driving forever. The road stretched out in front of them, glimmering in the distance, but there was nothing on either side as far as the eye could see. Just scrubby plants and miles of red dirt.

But then she spotted a sign in the distance. As they got closer, Elspeth could read that it said Starry Bay, with an arrow pointing to the right. Tunnock turned off the highway and slowed down, steering the car into a dusty main street. There was a line of houses and a battered old shop with the sign NELSON'S GENERAL STORE AND POST OFFICE outside it.

"I'll ask if anyone in that shop has seen my parents! Can you stop, please, Mr Tunnock?" Elspeth said. "You and Rory wait here."

She jumped out of the car and hurried across the street to the shop. She pushed open the door and stepped inside.

A large woman behind the till glanced up as Elspeth walked in, and when Elspeth smiled at her, the woman's mouth opened in amazement. She hurried out from behind the counter, pointing at Elspeth with a long, green-painted fingernail. A pile of bracelets on her arm tinkled as she moved.

"Well, I never. It's you!" she said, bending down to look at Elspeth. "You're that little girl who went missing! You're Elspeth Hart!" She gave Elspeth a gentle prod as if to check she was real. "You look

just like your mum. I'm Nellie, by the way.
Nellie Nelson."

"You've met my mum?" Elspeth started
speaking so quickly, she could hardly get
the words out fast enough. "Mum and Dad
were here, in Starry Bay?"

"Oh yes. They were here about a week
ago, love. Seemed very concerned, told me
all about you."

Nellie looked at Elspeth and her eyes were suddenly kind. "To be honest, I thought they'd be back by now. I've been wondering what happened to them."

"Back from *where*?" Elspeth asked. Her heart was thumping.

"The Never-ending Rainforest," Nellie Nelson said. "I made sure they had some food and decent camping gear, but I wonder if they got lost. I did warn them. The place is supposed to be haunted…"

Elspeth didn't want to waste another second. "Thank you," she said hurriedly. She hauled open the shop door, making the bell jingle loudly, but as she ran down the steps she heard a shout.

"Hey!" a voice cried. "You're that missing girl!"

Elspeth froze. She turned to see a bald

man sitting on the porch of the house next door to the shop, staring at her. He turned his head and shouted, "Belinda! Come out here! It's that runaway!"

The man got up and moved down the steps towards Elspeth. As he got nearer, Elspeth could see that his skin looked leathery and wrinkled, and there was a glint in his eye that she didn't like at all.

The door to the house behind him slammed and a skinny woman with grey hair in curlers came out on to the porch. "It won't be her, Bob," she was muttering. "You're imagining things…"

But when she saw Elspeth she stopped short. "It *is* her!" she yelled, her eyes lighting up. "You poor little mite, missing for all this time. Come on, my lovely, stay with us and we'll keep you safe. Come inside!"

"No, thank you," Elspeth said quickly, glancing over to where Tunnock and Rory were waiting.

She darted away across the street and got back into the Jeep as quickly as she could.

5
The Never-ending Rainforest Trail

"Mum and Dad *did* go into the rainforest," Elspeth told Tunnock and Rory as they drove off. "We have to go there, too!"

Rory had been looking at the map while she was in the shop. "There's a place called Crocodile Creek right next to the rainforest," he said. "Looks like it might have a campsite." He leaned forward and showed Elspeth the map.

"Great, let's head there. Maybe someone can take us to the start of the trail," Elspeth said. She glanced out of the window as they pulled away and saw the couple still standing on their porch, staring at her.

"What did those people want?" asked Rory.

"They'd seen my face on the posters," Elspeth replied. "They said I could stay in their house. I don't know why, but I got a very bad feeling from them."

"That's odd. They're still watching us," Rory said, wriggling around in the back so he could look out of the rear window.

Elspeth was relieved when they left the town and got back out on the open road.

As they drew close to the wilderness, they spotted a big falling-down sign.

It looked like an animal had chewed the edge of it and some of the letters were missing.

Tunnock followed the arrow on the sign, and the Jeep came to a halt in a clearing next to a big wooden house with a wonky-looking roof and leaves growing all over it. There were lots of smaller cabins dotted around it.

CR CODILE CREEK
NATURE RESER E
Daily wildlife tours
← Cabins to rent

The door to the big house slammed and a huge blond woman in yellow wellington boots marched towards them.

"You flaming galahs!" she shouted, gesturing at the Jeep. "You can't just drive in here without phoning ahead. You'll upset all the flipping crocodiles!"

"What's a flaming galah?" Rory whispered to Elspeth.

"Not sure, but it doesn't sound good. Stay there," Elspeth whispered back. She unfastened her seat belt and climbed out of the Jeep.

"I'm so sorry," Elspeth said. "We didn't mean to cause any trouble. We're looking for the trail into the Never-ending Rainforest. Can you help us?" She remembered how her parents had told her to shake hands when she met new people, so she held out her hand. "I'm Elspeth. That's my friend Rory in the car, and Mr Tunnock, who is looking after us."

Rory and Mr Tunnock climbed out of the Jeep, and the blond woman gave a grunt. Then she bent down to shake Elspeth's hand. Elspeth winced. It was like having her hand crushed in a vice.

"Uma Gumboots is the name," the woman said in a gruff voice. "But you can't get on that trail."

"Why not?" Elspeth asked.

"It's blocked," said Uma Gumboots in a matter-of-fact voice, scratching her armpit. "Storm damage. I'm working on rebuilding the path. It's not safe right now."

"Storm? When? Was anyone hurt?" Elspeth asked, her voice rising.

"Last week," said Uma Gumboots. "Nah, nobody got hurt. It just left a big old mess on the rainforest trail. Lots of rocks and trees to clear up."

"But I need to get into the rainforest!" Elspeth said. Then she realized Uma Gumboots was looking at her strangely. "It's just … we've come all the way from England!" she added.

"In a hurry, aintcha?" asked Uma Gumboots. "It'll be open again tomorrow or the next day."

"We could help you," said Elspeth with a

flash of inspiration. "Couldn't we? Perhaps we could stay here tonight?" She gestured at the little log cabins dotted around the big house. "Hire one of your cabins?"

Uma Gumboots looked Elspeth, Rory and Tunnock up and down. Then she shrugged her massive shoulders and gave a laugh.

"Well, alrighty," she said. "I won't charge you to stay if you help me clear that path. Those two cabins are available." She pointed towards two small cabins at the edge of the rainforest. "But you'll have to follow the house rules. No messing about, no talking after midnight, and DEFINITELY no making fun of the size of my feet."

Elspeth and Rory nodded and Elspeth took a sneaky look down at Uma Gumboots' feet. They were pretty huge. Tunnock gave a small bow, which seemed to please Uma Gumboots.

"We'll start work at six a.m. sharp tomorrow," Uma Gumboots said. "Meet me here. No excuses." Then she stomped back into the main house.

Elspeth gazed around Crocodile Creek Nature Reserve as Tunnock and Rory pulled their bags out of the Jeep. It looked like the main house had once been painted green, but now it was faded and cracked. There were rough paths leading away through the trees towards the smaller cabins, which were even more ramshackle than the big house.

When Elspeth and Rory stepped inside their cabin it was dusty and stuffy, and the roof above them sagged. Outside the window were thick green branches so overgrown that hardly any light was coming in. A parrot was sitting in the branches, staring at them curiously.

Rory clutched Lazlo tightly. "Do you trust Uma Gumboots, Elspeth?" he asked.

"I think we have to," Elspeth said, peering out of the window at the parrot. She could hear sounds she had never heard before … unfamiliar cheeps and chirps and birdcalls, and a kind of soft shushing noise as a little breeze shook the trees outside. The air smelled different, too.

Elspeth had butterflies in her tummy. She was in a strange new country and her parents were somewhere here as well. But could she find them in the dangerous rainforest?

6

Crocodile Creek Rules

Early the next morning, Elspeth and Rory hurried down the steps of their cabin just as Mr Tunnock came out of his. The door of the big house slammed loudly and Uma Gumboots came marching towards them with a grim expression on her face.

"Right!" she said, waving a large stick at them. "Crocodile Creek rules. No shouting, no fighting, no midnight feasts, no mucking about, no talking after eight p.m. and definitely no whining at any time. Got it?"

"Those are different rules from the ones she told us last night!" Rory whispered, but then Uma Gumboots gave them a sharp glare, and Elspeth and Rory nodded to show they had understood.

"You? Got it?" Uma Gumboots prodded Mr Tunnock with her stick. He was looking rather sweaty.

"Indeed, I understand," he said, wiping his brow.

"Before we clear the trail," Uma Gumboots said, "we gotta feed the crocs! Let's go!"

"Crocodiles!" hissed Rory, looking at Elspeth anxiously. He made sure Lazlo was tucked deep into his shirt pocket as they followed Uma Gumboots through the camp.

When they arrived at the crocodile pool, Elspeth was surprised to see they weren't the only people up this early. A boy and a girl about her age were there, too. The boy had spiky hair and pale skin, and the girl had a bright smile and shiny blond hair in bunches. They were both wearing red shorts and Crocodile Creek T-shirts.

"What are your names again? Elizabeth and Rory?" Uma asked as they marched towards the kids at the pool.

"It's Elspeth," Elspeth said. "Not Elizabeth."

"I'll just call you Elizabeth," Uma Gumboots said firmly, shoving a tree branch out of her way like it was nothing. She seemed incredibly strong. "Easier to remember. I had a dog called Elizabeth once. Lovely animal. Now, meet my nephew and niece, Jack and Fern. The twins are helping me out for a bit. Kids, meet Elizabeth, Rory and Mr Tunnock."

"Nice to meet you, Jack and Fern," Elspeth said. When Uma Gumboots was looking the other way she whispered, "My name's actually Elspeth!" and the twins gave her a smile in return.

Fern looked thoughtful. "Elspeth … that's an unusual name," she said. "I feel like I've seen it somewhere recently…"

"Enough of this chit-chat!" Uma Gumboots pointed to the water. "The crocs are up. Good to see you, my babies!"

Elspeth stared at the pool in amazement. What looked like large stones in the pool were starting to rise and move towards them. The crocodiles were huge and ancient-looking, and Elspeth gazed in wonder. Rory started nibbling his thumbnail nervously.

"Don't be scared," Fern whispered, leaning over towards Elspeth and Rory. "Auntie Uma's a bit nuts, but she knows a lot about animals, especially crocodiles. You won't get hurt." She looked at Elspeth intently. "Are you staying here long?"

"Not sure yet," Elspeth said carefully.

She didn't know how much she should give away.

"House rule number three!" shouted
Uma Gumboots, waving fish at them. "No
secret whispering! You ankle-biters can
go and get some shovels for Elizabeth and
Rory and Mr T here. We're going to finish
clearing the rainforest trail this morning."
She took a strange-looking device from one
of her many pockets and flipped it open to
show Mr Tunnock. It looked a bit like a tin

of sardines, but all sorts of funny things stuck out from it when Uma pressed various buttons.

"See this, Mr T? It's a Fix-It-Mate tool. I invented it myself. It's an eight-in-one hammer, knife, spoon, fork, drill, compass, toothbrush and torch. Clever, eh?" She nudged Mr Tunnock with her elbow so hard that he almost fell over.

"Most ingenious," said Mr Tunnock, looking slightly frightened.

"Come on!" Fern said. "On the way to the tool shed, we'll show you the kangaroos and koalas. And if you're lucky we might see an emu roaming about!"

Elspeth wanted more than anything to get into the rainforest, but then Fern pointed out a large paddock, and for a second she forgot all about her parents.

"Wow!" Elspeth said.

The paddock was full of kangaroos. They were huge – much taller than she was. They leaped around on their strong hind legs, but Elspeth thought their faces looked friendly.

Jack opened the gate and went in, feeding some of the kangaroos by hand, while Elspeth and Rory leaned on the fence and watched with wide eyes.

"Jack's afraid of nothing," Fern said, as he hugged one of the kangaroos. "Sometimes he does the craziest stuff."

"Are you older, or is Jack?" Rory asked.

"Oh, I'm the oldest!" said Fern. "I was born two whole minutes before him. We used to look identical when we were little, then I grew taller than Jack. He doesn't like that much!" She laughed. "We live in

Brisbane, but we're on school holidays just now. We love staying here, even though Auntie Uma makes us work hard! Come and meet the koalas. They're really cool."

Elspeth liked the koalas even more than the kangaroos. They had fluffy ears and sweet faces and most of them were dozing, apart from one who was chewing a eucalyptus leaf. Even Rory petted it without being worried.

"Auntie Uma's setting up a koala hospital," Jack explained. "If the place doesn't close down first. Not many visitors come here. People say it's too old-fashioned. There's nobody staying at the moment."

"Nobody at all?" Elspeth said. That explained why the reserve was so quiet.

"Nope. It's like a ghost town!" Jack said, opening up a big shed and handing out shovels. "That's why she needs our help. She can't afford to pay proper staff!" Then he looked at Elspeth more closely. "Hey, you look sort of … familiar." He frowned. "I'm trying to think…"

"…who you look like." Fern finished Jack's sentence. "Wait, I know! You're the girl from the 'missing' posters we saw in town!"

"Yes!" Jack said. "You're Elspeth Hart, aren't you?"

Elspeth paused, but she knew there was no point lying when her face was on posters all over town. So she told Jack and Fern about being kidnapped, and how Miss Crabb was after her family's top-secret sticky toffee sauce recipe. And how Elspeth and Rory were on a mission to track down Elspeth's mum and dad. Jack and Fern listened in silence, paying attention to every word.

"So, you see, I *have* to get into the Never-ending Rainforest," Elspeth finished. "My parents went in over a week ago! Anything could have happened to them by now!"

"I heard there's a pack of wild kangaroos in there, and that they attack anyone who goes near them. You can hear them howling at night. I don't want to scare you, Elspeth," said Jack, "but that place is SERIOUSLY dangerous."

7
Another Seriously Dangerous Place

Meanwhile, Miss Crabb was driving a rusty
old van through Port Bongo as fast as it
could go. On top of the van there was a sign
saying MEAT PIES, with a plastic meat pie
next to it. Miss Crabb had stolen the pie
van as soon as she and Gladys got off the
cargo ship, and she felt very smug because
it was an excellent hiding place – they could

sleep in the van as well as travel in it. Miss Crabb put her foot down, going so fast that the van started veering from side to side.

"Ooh, I feel car sick!" said Gladys Goulash, who had eaten a dozen meat pies for breakfast.

"Oh, shut up, you greasy gibbon," said Miss Crabb, screeching round the corner and stopping in a creepy alleyway. "This is where I'm going to get everything I need for catching Elspeth Hart!"

They were outside what looked like an abandoned shop. There were boards over most of the windows and someone had painted NASTY PETS R US above the door in messy letters.

"It's like a pet shop, but for baddies," Miss Crabb explained, getting out of the van. "Wait here, Gladys Goulash."

Miss Crabb gave the shop door a kick and it swung open. She stepped inside and looked around happily. "This is JUST my kind of place," she said.

The shop was gloomy and dark, with only a single light bulb dangling from the ceiling. A huge tank full of angry piranhas and vicious sea snakes bubbled in one corner. Another tank held hundreds of big spiders and there were some scorpions having a fight in a third. It was, dear reader, probably the creepiest pet shop in the world.

"I need some Australian Bitey Bitey spiders," Miss Crabb said to the man behind the desk. "Lots of them."

The man slicked back his greasy hair and twiddled his moustache.

"Great choice, the Australian Bitey Biteys," he said. "Nasty critters, they are. One bite from them and you feel sick. Two bites and your face turns green. Three bites and you start talking in riddles. Painful, too. They're a dollar each."

"Perfect," Miss Crabb said. "I'll take a hundred." She had stolen all the money from the till inside the pie van, so she had plenty to spend. She looked around with her sharp eyes as the greasy man went to fetch the spiders. Her eye fell on a huge net. It looked almost twice as tall as her.

"What's that?" she asked, pointing at it when the greasy man came back.

"Whale net," the man said, handing her a box that was making a horrible rattling noise. "They're massive. Very strong. You could trap an elephant in one of those."

Miss Crabb narrowed her eyes. "Yes…
I think I'll have one. Just in case," she said.
She paid for her purchases and got back in
the van. Gladys Goulash was fast asleep
with her mouth hanging open and drool
running down her chin.

"Put this in your rucksack," Miss Crabb
ordered, shoving the box towards her so
Gladys woke up with a snort.

Miss Crabb drove as fast as possible
towards Starry Bay. She only slowed down
when she spotted a notice stuck on a lamp
post on the outskirts of the town.

"What's that I see?" Miss Crabb said. She
wound down her window and stared at the
poster with Elspeth's face on it. "Ha," she
crowed. "Just like I said. Those idiot parents
have been here already. Elspeth's bound to
turn up, too."

"OOH," Gladys Goulash said. "There's a reward. Why don't we just nab Elspeth and then we'll get that money?"

"Don't be such a nincompoop!" hissed Miss Crabb. "That reward's only a thousand dollars. We'll make MILLIONS when we get that Extra-special Sticky Toffee Sauce recipe from Elspeth again. Besides, it's not winning if I deliver her back to her parents. I want to make that little rat miserable."

Miss Crabb drove further up the road and parked outside Nelson's General Store.

"I've got to get some water. You stay here and DON'T EAT ANY MORE PIES."

Miss Crabb clambered out of the van, adjusted her sun hat, and stepped inside the shop, wiping the sweat off her forehead.

Nellie Nelson leaned back and covered her nose at the smell from Miss Crabb's vest. She uncovered it when Miss Crabb came to the till with a big bottle of water.

"Well now, I haven't seen you around here before," Mrs Nelson said. "Welcome to Starry Bay! I'm Nellie. Nellie Nelson. What's your name, love?"

"Hello," said Miss Crabb in her best fake-nice voice. "My name is … Agnes Mince." She grinned, showing her dirty false teeth.

"Nice to meet you, Miss Mince," said Nellie. "Are you on holiday here?"

"Not exactly," said Miss Crabb. She paid for the bottle of water quickly and turned to leave. "Must hurry."

Nellie Nelson bustled forward and held the door open for her, craning her neck to see where Miss Crabb would go. She spotted the pie van at once.

"Oh, is that your van, Miss Mince?" she

asked. "Everyone here loves meat pies. I'll spread the word you're in town. You'll have plenty of hungry customers."

"Gah!" Miss Crabb muttered under her breath. She didn't want to serve up meat pies – she wanted to lie low and wait for Elspeth Hart. But it was too late. Mrs Nelson had stepped outside and was shouting over to her neighbours.

"Bob! Belinda! Some visitors are in town selling fresh meat pies, isn't that great?"

"Wowsers!" said Bob. He waved at another man passing through town. "Hey, Scotty, meat pies! Tell your mates!"

It wasn't often that new and exciting things happened in Starry Bay, and in twenty minutes there was a long queue outside the van. Miss Crabb and Gladys Goulash quickly sold all the pies they

had, which wasn't many, because Gladys
Goulash had eaten so many of them.

"We could make some more lovely pies
with rats' legs and mouse droppings, like
we did when we worked in that school,"
Gladys Goulash said, licking gravy off her
nose.

Miss Crabb wasn't paying attention. She
was listening carefully to a couple of women
who were chatting as they ate their pies.

"Yeah, Nellie Nelson said that poor
little Elspeth Hart girl is in town," one of
them was saying. "She saw her heading off
towards Crocodile Creek."

"Aw, poor girl," said the other one. "Her
folks went into the rainforest, didn't they?
She'll never find them now."

A frown spread over Miss Crabb's face.
She pulled down the shutter on the van,

then turned to Gladys Goulash and flared her nostrils.

"Elspeth Hart is here already! How did that little ratbag get to Australia before us?" Miss Crabb raged. "She's just a titchy little kid! I thought we were one step ahead of her!"

She threw a plate of cold gravy at Gladys Goulash in anger. It made her feel a bit better to see Gladys Goulash with a big gravy stain down the front of her vest.

"Never mind," she said. "I've got my Bitey Bitey spiders, I've got a huge net to catch people in and I know where that brat Elspeth is staying. I'm ready. We're going to Crocodile Creek RIGHT NOW."

8
The Trail Appears

"Right!" shouted Uma Gumboots. "Animals fed – time to clear the trail!" She marched ahead of Elspeth, Rory, Jack, Fern and Mr Tunnock, leading them to a pile of muddy rocks and leaves even taller than Elspeth.

"This is going to be a lot of work," muttered Rory, gazing up at the blockage. Lazlo stuck a cautious head out of Rory's

shirt pocket, took one look around, and hid
in his pocket again.

"Get moving!" bellowed Uma Gumboots.
"Jack and Fern, you climb up there and start
passing rocks down to Rory. Rory, you hand
them to Elizabeth, and then Mr T and I
will carry them over to my truck. Get those
muscles working, Mr T!" She slapped Mr
Tunnock on the arm and smiled at him,
making the butler blush.

"I think Auntie Uma really likes Mr
Tunnock," Jack whispered. "Maybe she
wants him to be her boyfriend!"

Rory's eyes widened in horror and
Elspeth laughed, forgetting her worries for
a minute.

The work was hard, especially in the
heat. There was no breeze to cool them
down and Elspeth could feel her dress

sticking to her. She wished she was wearing shorts like Jack and Fern. Bugs flew around their heads and the rocks were heavy. After a few hours, Elspeth was starting to wonder if they would ever get the trail clear.

Once or twice she looked over to see Mr Tunnock stopping for a break and to wipe his face. He'd gone very pink, but every time he paused, Uma Gumboots gave him a big slap on the shoulder and told him to get back to it.

They worked all day, only stopping at lunchtime for some ouga ouga fruit and water, which Uma produced from the back of her truck. Elspeth couldn't bear the smell of the ouga ouga fruit, but once she was actually chewing it, it tasted OK – a bit like a pear.

Jack pushed his hair off his face with a sweaty arm. "Thank goodness for a break. Auntie Uma makes us work like slaves!"

But as they ate, Elspeth pictured her parents in the middle of the awful storm, cowering as a big tree came down next to them. She shook her head.

Don't let your imagination run away with you, she told herself.

Suddenly there was a shrill ringing sound from Uma Gumboots' pocket.

"G'day, Nellie Nelson!" Uma Gumboots was shouting into the phone. "Speak up, mate, the line's a bit crackly. What's that? Meat pies? We'll be there. Save us some!"

She stuffed the phone back in one of the pockets of her shorts. "Good news!" she said, waving her Fix-It-Mate tool in the air. "Some woman called Agnes Mince has turned up in Starry Bay, selling meat pies. I'm going in to buy some for our dinner. Mr T, you can come with me, keep me company. Who wants one?"

"No, thanks," Elspeth said at once, her thoughts still focused on clearing the path as quickly as possible. Then she looked up. "Did you say … *Agnes* Mince?" she asked.

"That's the one," Uma Gumboots said. "Nellie Nelson reckons she's a mean-looking sheila, but she's come to town in a van with another woman, and they're selling good hot pies. Pommies, apparently."

"Pommies means they're English, doesn't it?" Elspeth asked Fern in a low voice, and Fern nodded.

A chill went through her. *Two English women turning up out of the blue ... and Agnes is Miss Crabb's middle name,* she thought. Elspeth gazed after Uma Gumboots as she stomped off to her truck, slinging an arm around Mr Tunnock. Then she turned to Rory, her eyes worried.

"I think it's Crabb and Goulash," she said. "I can't be certain, but I know Agnes is Crabb's middle name. She might have picked it if she had to make up a fake name."

"Oh no," Rory whispered. "I bet you're right."

"That poster of me ... it said my parents had a tip-off," Elspeth said slowly.

Rory followed her train of thought. "Yes,

Miss Crabb probably tipped them off. She wanted them out of the way, so she sent them to the rainforest."

Elspeth swallowed, her throat suddenly dry. "Crabb knows that I'd come looking for Mum and Dad. That's why she's here. She's after me."

"What?" Fern gasped. "That evil Crabb woman's here, in Starry Bay?"

"Yes!" Elspeth said. "So I need to get into that rainforest and find my parents before she catches me again."

"But it's going to get dark in a few hours, Elspeth," Jack interrupted. "If you're doing this, you need to go tomorrow morning. And you and Rory can't go alone."

He turned to his sister, and she nodded.

"We'll go with you," the twins said in unison.

"Are you sure?" said Elspeth.

The first part of the trail should be OK,"
Fern said. "We walked that route once with
Auntie Uma. But we can't go beyond the
waterfall. After the waterfall, the path leads
to the Lost Valley. Nobody dares go there."

"L-Lost Valley?" stammered Rory. "I don't
like the sound of that."

"What's in the Lost Valley?" Elspeth
asked.

"Nobody knows," Jack said. "There are all sorts of rumours … that it's haunted, that there's a big bog that's actually quicksand… People who've gone there have heard horrible noises. Like a kind of howling or crying."

Elspeth shivered. It sounded awful. But if her parents were in the rainforest, there was no time to lose.

"You'll need some camping gear," Jack said. "There's plenty in the tool shed. Grab a tent, binoculars and some waterproofs. And some insect repellent, or you'll get bitten to pieces…"

Elspeth listened carefully to Jack's list. She was frightened, but secretly she knew she would go as far as she had to, if it meant finding her parents.

Even if she ended up in the Lost Valley.

9

A Nasty Surprise

That evening, Rory went to check on
Tunnock, who had come back from town
with Uma Gumboots looking a bit pink and
needing a lie-down.

"I'll get our camping things ready for
tomorrow morning," Elspeth said, as Rory
headed over to Mr Tunnock's cabin. She
was on red alert as she walked towards the

tool shed. Every little sound was making her jump. With Miss Crabb in the area, she couldn't be too careful.

Elspeth stepped into the shed and started digging through the piles of boots and waterproofs. Then she heard a sharp crack outside, like someone standing on a twig. She froze, her heart pounding, hardly daring to breathe. She stayed very still in one spot for what felt like ages and ages, until there was another crack outside and a soft crunching sound.

Whoever it was must have gone.

Elspeth let out a long sigh of relief. She grabbed the camping gear and tiptoed cautiously out of the shed. She looked left and right – there was nobody about. She turned to close the latch, fumbling to do it as quickly as possible.

But as she did, somebody grabbed her and dragged her backwards, clapping a hand over her mouth so she couldn't scream.

Elspeth dropped everything she was carrying and struggled with all her strength, but the person in the dark was stronger. She was thrown into the back of a van, and the doors slammed and locked behind her.

"HELP! SOMEONE HELP ME!" Elspeth screamed as loudly as she could, but it was no use. The van started moving and she was alone in the darkness.

Miss Crabb had her at last.

Elspeth's eyes filled with tears, but she told herself to be calm. "Focus," she said to herself. "Try to listen carefully for sounds outside. You need to know where they're taking you."

She stopped kicking and stood in the van as it rocked from side to side, but all she could hear was the roar of the engine. They turned left, then right, then left again, and Elspeth started to lose hope.

She took big deep breaths. *Rory will worry when I don't come back soon*, she told herself. *He can get Uma Gumboots to help.* But as the van rattled over a bumpy road, Elspeth knew Miss Crabb would have taken her far, far away before anyone came looking for her.

Finally the van came to a sharp stop,

throwing Elspeth to the floor.

She scrambled up as quickly as she could.
She heard a door slam and footsteps outside
coming closer. She looked around; was there
anything she could use as a weapon? Could
she clunk Miss Crabb over the head and
escape? But there was nothing. The van was
completely empty.

There was the sound of the door being
unlocked and Elspeth crouched, ready to
try and make a run for it. The creaky doors
opened and someone shone a torch right
at her. Elspeth blinked and screwed up her
eyes against the bright light.

"Out you get, little girl," said a voice.
And when Elspeth opened her eyes, she got
the shock of her life.

It wasn't Miss Crabb and Gladys
Goulash at all.

10
Not Miss Crabb At All

It was the bald man from the house next to Nelson's General Store.

"We're not gonna hurt you," the man said. He was wearing a wide-brimmed hat with corks around it, so Elspeth couldn't see his eyes. The sour-faced woman was standing next to him. She still had the curlers in. Elspeth felt a jolt of panic in her chest. What did they want?

"Don't worry, little girl," the woman said, in a sweet voice that Elspeth knew was fake. She smiled at Elspeth, showing two missing teeth.

You can always tell, dear reader, when a grown-up doesn't like you. You can see it in their eyes, even if they are smiling.

"What do you want with me?" Elspeth said. There was a little tremble in her voice, but she stood up as straight as she could.

"I'm Belinda and this is my husband, Bob, and we just want to help you, dear," the woman went on. She moved towards Elspeth, but Elspeth jumped back at once.

"We know your parents are looking for you and we'd like to make sure you're safe when they arrive," Belinda said. "We thought you could stay in our … holiday cabin."

"You don't even know where my parents are!" Elspeth said. She couldn't keep the fear out of her voice. "You can't keep me here!"

"Aw, what a shame," Belinda said, and her voice was suddenly mean. "Bob, let's get Elspeth into her new home."

Elspeth jumped out of the van and tried to run, but Bob grabbed her at once. She squirmed and kicked as hard as she could, but Bob was much stronger than she was.

"Noooo! Let me GO!" Elspeth screamed

at the top of her lungs, but there was nothing around them – no houses or people or roads. Nobody to come to her rescue.

Bob hauled her through the darkness and shoved her into an old wooden shack. The door slammed, and Elspeth heard the sound of it being bolted shut, then the sound of the van doors closing.

"There's plenty of water in there!" Bob shouted, as the engine started up. "We'll check on you in a few days. Enjoy your stay!" There was a sound of horrible fake laughing as the van zoomed off.

"Come back!" Elspeth shouted. She started banging on the door with all her strength. "Let me OOOOOUUUT!" But after a few minutes, she knew nobody was coming.

When she stopped banging on the door, Elspeth noticed that it was eerily quiet outside. She could hear nothing except the sound of crickets. As her eyes adjusted to the darkness, Elspeth could see a big bottle of water in one corner of the room, and an old sheet on the floor. Nothing else. The floor was made of dirt, and the whole cabin looked rickety, but when Elspeth kicked at the walls, they were sturdy and wouldn't budge. The door was securely bolted. There wasn't even a window.

For the first time in over a year, Elspeth sat down on the floor and cried. She had got so close to finding her parents. She had escaped from an awful school, hidden on a cruise ship, travelled all over the world and she'd outsmarted Miss Crabb time after time. But now she was trapped … when her parents might only be a few miles away. Elspeth couldn't bear it.

She cried and cried until her face was puffy and she got the hiccups. And then she stopped crying and started thinking.

"There has to be a way out of here," she muttered, walking around her little prison again. "This isn't the end. There HAS to be a way out."

11
No Way Out

Elspeth tried wriggling her hand under the door, but it only got a little way and then got stuck.

After that, Elspeth sat in a corner of the cabin, racking her brains for a clever escape plan and coming up with nothing. All through the night, Elspeth thought about the mystery stories she had read in the

Pandora Pants School for Show-offs. She was trying to remember the adventures she had read, where smart children had escaped from nasty places.

She took a sip of her water. It was warm and tasted awful, but Elspeth knew it was precious. She would need to keep drinking it in the heat, or she could get very ill.

Then, just as it started to get light, Elspeth remembered something she'd read in a story long ago. She looked at the water bottle she was still holding. Then she looked at the dirt floor of the hut.

"I wonder…" Elspeth said aloud. She poured a tiny bit of water on to the dirt next to the door, and then scraped it with her hands. The dirt turned to a kind of sludge and Elspeth managed to scoop away a handful quite easily. She stared at it in excitement, then scrabbled at the sludge some more. Soon there was a space under the door big enough to push her arm through.

If I keep pouring on water and then scooping away the dirt, I might be able to crawl through there! she thought. But then she paused. What if she used up all her water, but couldn't make a hole big enough? She didn't want to be stuck in the hot cabin for days without a drink.

But as she sat there, hearing nothing outside but crickets, Elspeth knew she had to try. She started pouring water and scooping at the dirt, getting messier and messier, and more and more hot and sticky. It took an awfully long time, but when there was just a tiny trickle of water left, Elspeth Hart was able to shimmy down into the hole she had dug. She lowered one leg into the hole, hunched over and made herself as small as she could. She had to wriggle and squirm, and she scraped her back on the door as she squeezed under it.

But finally, with a great big push, she clambered out of the muddy hole on the other side of the door.

She was free!

Elspeth wiped the sweat off her forehead with a grubby hand and looked around. Next to the little cabin was a single dirt track. But which way should she go, left or right? Around her were miles and miles of flat reddish land and dried-up looking trees.

Elspeth had read about the Australian outback – miles and miles of empty land where people could get horribly lost and never find their way home.

"How can I work out which way to go?" she asked herself. She took a deep breath and tried to calm herself down. Then she walked along the track a little way, looking at it carefully. In one direction there were no marks on it – nothing at all.

Elspeth walked the other way.

"Yes!" she said out loud. She could just make out faint tyre prints. That must be the way back to town.

There was nothing else for it. Elspeth started walking. She felt like running, but she knew she needed to save her energy. Every so often she turned around to make sure there was nobody behind her. She knew that even if Bob and Belinda didn't show up, Miss Crabb might appear at any second.

12
Miss Crabb Creeps Around

Of course, dear reader, Miss Crabb and Gladys Goulash did not know that Elspeth had been carried away by Bob and Belinda. Miss Crabb thought Elspeth was still in Crocodile Creek, and she was feeling very excited about hunting her down and luring her into a big pit full of spiders. Miss Crabb and Gladys Goulash waited until it was dark, then they drove their pie van to the edge of Crocodile Creek Nature Reserve and parked up in an overgrown bush.

"We'll find out where Elspeth Hart is sleeping, Gladys Goulash," said Miss Crabb, "and the second she goes off into the rainforest to find her soppy parents, we'll follow her. Eee-hee-hee!"

"Yeah! Then we'll catch them all and EAT THEM!" Gladys Goulash said, getting carried away.

"We're not eating anybody, you nincompoop!" Miss Crabb said. She did a little dance of rage. "Enough of your stupid ideas. You're only here to carry my stuff. Follow me and shut up."

It was very dark in Crocodile Creek. Miss Crabb had an old torch she'd found in the van, but it was running out of battery

and only gave a weak light. She scuttled
through the bushes next to the main house,
with Gladys Goulash crashing after her.

Miss Crabb crept up to the window
and peered in. She could see a huge blond
woman talking to a tall, thin man who was
biting his nails. But there was no sign of
Elspeth Hart.

"Gah! Where is she? Where's that little pile of poo?" Miss Crabb muttered. She scurried away towards the cabins. "She's around here somewhere, I know it!"

They peered in the windows of several cabins, but couldn't see Elspeth anywhere. Finally, in a very bad mood, Miss Crabb marched up to the last cabin on the edge of the reserve. She stuck her pointy nose up over the window ledge and sneaked a look. Then she nodded in satisfaction.

She could see Rory talking to Jack and Fern, who were looking very worried. Rory was putting on socks and boots as if he was about to go outside. Lazlo was bopping up and down on Rory's shoulder, but Miss Crabb couldn't hear what they were saying.

"Bingo," she said. "There's that idiotic boy, Rory Snitter, and some other stupid children.

Elspeth can't be far away. We'll camp out here, Gladys Goulash." Miss Crabb moved away from the path and started burrowing her way into some thick bushes.

"Ooh, but I don't want to sleep out here! What about the critters?" Gladys Goulash said anxiously. "Big spiders! Scorpions! It's even worse than sleeping in the cargo hold of that plane! Can't we go back to the van?"

"Knickers to that," said Miss Crabb scornfully. "Someone might notice the van. Much better to hide out here. Anyway, I can squash a spider or a scorpion, no matter how big they are. I'm not scared." She curled her arms around her legs, and leaned her head up against a tree trunk. Then she thought of something and sat up again.

"So long as there aren't any koalas." Miss Crabb looked around, then gave a shudder.

"Horrible cuddly, fluffy things. Can't stand them. You take the first watch, Gladys Goulash."

And with that, Miss Crabb fell asleep and started snoring.

Gladys Goulash did as she was told, sitting up next to Miss Crabb, clutching their binoculars with one hand and nervously picking her nose with the other.

13
The Hunt Begins

By the time Elspeth reached Crocodile Creek, she was dizzy with exhaustion and her feet ached. The mud had dried in her hair and on her clothes, and she could feel her scalp starting to burn in the sun.

Rory and Tunnock shot out of the main house as soon as they spotted her, followed by Jack and Fern. Rory threw his arm around Elspeth and helped her to a seat on the porch.

"Elspeth!" he cried. "I thought Miss Crabb had got you! We've been out all night looking for you!"

"Water…" was all Elspeth could say. She was weak from walking so far in the heat.

"I'll get some," Mr Tunnock said, hurrying off.

"Aunt Uma's been driving around for hours, searching for you," Jack told Elspeth. "Don't worry, she's not going to go to the cops. She doesn't trust the police."

"Yes, I had to tell Uma Gumboots who we were, and I told her about Miss Crabb, too," Rory said anxiously. "I'm sorry, I know you didn't want any more grown-ups involved. We searched for Miss Crabb and Gladys Goulash, but we only found their van and it was empty. Where did they take you?"

Before Elspeth could reply, Uma Gumboots came marching towards them. She scooped Elspeth up with one arm and carried her inside the house, plonking her down on a couch. The others crowded round and Mr Tunnock brought Elspeth cool orange squash to drink.

"Flipping kids getting kidnapped and

disturbing the crocs!" Uma said. "Your mate Rory here told me all about this Miss Crabb woman."

Elspeth shook her head. "It wasn't Miss Crabb who took me," she said, as soon as she could speak. She swallowed some more squash — it was cold and delicious. "It was Bob and Belinda, the couple who live next to Nelson's General Store. They must have wanted the reward money." Elspeth explained how she'd managed to escape.

"Well I never! I'll teach them to go around kidnapping kids," Uma Gumboots said, putting her giant hands on her hips. "I'll go and see them right now!"

"There's no time!" Elspeth said. "Miss Crabb is around here somewhere and she's after me. I've got to get into the Never-ending Rainforest and find my parents before she catches me!"

"Well…" Uma Gumboots switched on a fan to cool Elspeth down and looked at her thoughtfully. "You might be all right by this arvo, if you rest." She turned to Mr Tunnock. "Mr T, if these ankle-biters are heading into the rainforest, I'd better go with them. Could you stay and keep an eye on the animals here? You're a good bloke, very neat and tidy, I trust you."

Mr Tunnock looked nervous. "I would be honoured," he said. "Only, I solemnly promised Master Rory's parents that I would stay with him at all times."

"It's all right, Tunnock," Rory said. "We'll be fine with Uma Gumboots."

"I'm not sure that I—" Mr Tunnock began, but Uma Gumboots wouldn't let him finish.

"You're not too good in the heat, Mr T,"
Uma Gumboots said firmly. "You'll be much
more use here. Keep an eye on things and
stay in the shade when you can." She threw
an arm around Mr Tunnock and ruffled his
hair, making him give a tiny squeak of fear.
"I'll look after Rory and Elizabeth."

"It's not Elizabeth, it's Els…" Elspeth
started saying, then she decided it wasn't
worth it. She lay back on the couch and
closed her eyes, trying to push away the
memory of the horrible cabin. She'd need all
her strength this afternoon.

"RIGHT! Rainforest rules," shouted Uma
Gumboots a few hours later. Elspeth was
feeling much better, and everyone was
packed up and ready to go. "No mucking

about, no wandering off by yourself, no sticking spiders in my sleeping bag and no talking after midnight. Got it?"

"Got it!" said Elspeth, Rory, Jack and Fern.

They waved to Mr Tunnock, who was cleaning the windows of the main house, and they headed into the Never-ending Rainforest.

Elspeth's heart pounded as they walked along the trail. She had thought the rainforest would be a peaceful place, but the air was filled with the sound of little rushing streams and the steady *plink-plink* of drops falling from the trees. She was glad to be wearing waterproofs as the rain pattered down. Jack and Fern pointed out birds and brightly coloured butterflies to Rory, but Elspeth was focused on looking around for clues as they walked.

After about an hour, when the trees became more dense and dark around them, Elspeth gave a cry of excitement.

"They've been here! Mum and Dad have definitely been here!" she said, grabbing Rory's arm. Stuck on a branch around the height of Elspeth's head was a bright red and silver sweet wrapper. Elspeth plucked it from the branch and held it up.

"'Hart's Fine Sweets'," Rory read, peering at the wrapper. "That's amazing! We're definitely on the right track!"

Elspeth grinned at him. They were getting nearer. "Maybe they left these wrappers as a sort of trail, in case they got lost," she said. She held the wrapper in her hand for a minute, then stuck it back on the branch. As they walked on, Elspeth kept looking out for more wrappers, and soon she spotted a second, then a third. With every wrapper, Elspeth felt more hopeful.

After a couple of hours, Uma Gumboots made everyone stop for a break.

"Tucker time!" she said, pouring some cold beans into a pan and throwing in what looked like a handful of grubs.

"Oh, please can we keep going?" Elspeth asked. She was hot and tired, but she couldn't bear the thought of wasting any more time. "What if my parents have gone past the waterfall, into the Lost Valley?"

But Uma Gumboots stayed firm.

"Eat!" she said. "Rainforest rules! Eat some tucker and keep your strength up."

Elspeth sighed, but she knew it was no good arguing. She swallowed some cold beans and drank some water.

"Perhaps we should have someone on

guard whenever we stop?" Elspeth said. "Rory and I can go first. We'll keep our eyes and ears open in case Miss Crabb appears."

"Good plan, Elizabeth," said Uma Gumboots, throwing a handful of grubs into her mouth.

Elspeth and Rory moved a little way from the others and sat down on some rocks at the edge of the path, listening carefully for any unusual sounds.

Rory picked up his binoculars and scanned the trees around them.

"Do you hear anything?" he asked.

Elspeth paused for a moment, listening, then shook her head. They sat quietly for a bit and Elspeth gazed out into the close, hot jumble of trees. *Where are you, Mum and Dad?* she wondered.

Then they heard a cracking sound.

14
Suspicious
Cracking Sounds

Miss Crabb and Gladys Goulash were
not the only dangerous people creeping
around the rainforest. Bob and Belinda
were sure that Elspeth was still locked in
their hut, and they'd also headed into the
rainforest looking for her parents. They
were determined to get their hands on
the reward money. Bob's money-making

schemes never went very well. This year, he'd already lost hundreds of dollars betting in a sheep-shearing competition, so he was VERY keen to find Elspeth's parents. And he even had a secret route into the rainforest that nobody else knew about.

"My grandfather told me about this track," Bob said to Belinda. "Nobody knows about it, not a soul! We'll find those parents in no time!" He slapped his big belly and put on his hat with corks dangling from it, and they trudged out of Starry Bay and along a dried-up riverbed.

"This better be worth it, Bob!" Belinda said impatiently. She swatted flies out of her face as they went.

They clambered through the trees for a long time, then came to a huge, bad-smelling swamp.

"We just have to get through this small patch of mud, my darling," said Bob in a cheerful voice.

"You drongo, Bob!" Belinda hissed. "That's not a small patch of mud, that's a stinking great swamp! There could be crocodiles in there!"

"It'll be worth it, my darling! We'll get the reward money much quicker this way," Bob said greedily. "Can't imagine Elspeth Hart's parents have gone very far. We'll just have to go through this, uh … muddy bit, then we'll come out close to the waterfall."

He took a big squelchy step into the swamp.

"We'd better find 'em, Bob!" shrieked Belinda, as she slithered after him, holding her nose with one hand.

"Come on!" Bob said, ignoring his wife's

sour face. They came to the edge of the
swamp and Bob hauled himself out, then
offered a hand to Belinda. She grabbed it,
tried to climb up and fell back with a shriek,
taking Bob with her. They landed in the
swamp with a loud plopping sound.

"You dingbat, get me outta here!" shrieked Belinda, flapping around in the mud. They both floundered in the swamp until Bob shoved Belinda up on to the bank ahead of him and scrambled out himself.

In fact, dear reader, although Bob and Belinda were sweaty and covered in sludge and not getting along very well, their shortcut had worked. In a few minutes they had found the rainforest trail, and they were actually ahead of Elspeth and Rory's camp.

Bob stopped and plonked himself down on a rock to rest.

"Told ya I'd find the trail!" he said proudly. "We'll stop here, get some grub and have a break."

Way back on the trail, Miss Crabb and Gladys Goulash were squelching through the rainforest, following the tracks that Elspeth and her friends had left. They didn't have proper waterproofs, so they were both wearing old carrier bags, and Gladys Goulash was stopping every so often to rub her bum. It was very sore where a scorpion had stung it during the night. Her shoulders were sore, too, because Miss Crabb was making her carry a huge rucksack containing the box of spiders, the huge net, a tent, all their water and a huge jar of pickled eggs – Miss Crabb's favourite snack.

Miss Crabb paused in her squelchy walk and put the binoculars to her eyes.

"Excellent," she said smugly. "I can see stupid Elspeth. Though I don't like the look of that big blond woman." Miss Crabb trained her binoculars on Uma Gumboots. "Might need to get rid of her before I nab the girl. Adults are more pesky than children. They're harder to squash!" And she gave a nasty laugh.

Miss Crabb paused to think for a moment. The blond woman was as tall as she was and almost twice as wide.

Then Miss Crabb took a crafty look at Gladys Goulash. Gladys Goulash was short, but she was heavy. In fact, Miss Crabb thought, Gladys Goulash would make an excellent weapon.

Miss Crabb could see the blond woman piling some spoons into a dirty pan. Miss Crabb strained to hear as Uma Gumboots shouted over to the children. "I'm going to wash these down at the creek. No mucking about while I'm gone!"

"Come on, Gladys Goulash," said Miss Crabb. She hurried towards the creek and stopped a little way from the water, where Uma couldn't see them.

"Get up that tree," Miss Crabb ordered, shoving Gladys Goulash ahead of her. Gladys climbed on to a low branch and then stopped.

"I don't want to!" she said. "I don't like being up high!"

"Gah!" Miss Crabb shoved Gladys Goulash's bum as hard as she could. "Get up there or I'll put a frog down your vest. Hurry up."

Very clumsily, Gladys Goulash climbed up the tree with Miss Crabb right behind her.

"When that blond woman comes along here, you're going to jump on her," said Miss Crabb.

"WHAT?" shouted Gladys Goulash.

"Oh, don't be so pathetic," said Miss Crabb. "You jump on her, squash her, and then I'll climb down and tie her up. We'll drag her into the bushes and leave her there! Eee-hee-hee!"

"But … but … don't we want to catch

Elspeth and get the recipe?" asked Gladys Goulash.

"Yes, you baboon, we do," said Miss Crabb. "But this way, we get the big grown-up out of the way so she doesn't cause us any trouble. Now, you shurrup before she hears you."

Uma Gumboots was almost at the creek. She was stomping along carrying the dirty pan and spoons and humming to herself. As she got close to the tree where they were hiding, Miss Crabb gave Gladys Goulash a prod. "Get ready to jump," she said. "Three seconds, Gladys Goulash."

"Nooo," moaned Gladys Goulash, clutching on to the branches tightly. "I don't want to!"

Uma Gumboots was only a few metres away. Miss Crabb lost her temper.

"Get out of the tree and squash her NOW!" she shouted, and she shoved Gladys Goulash with all her strength.

"Waaaaaah!" screeched Gladys Goulash, and she dropped from the tree like a very large and stinky cannonball.

Uma Gumboots looked up in horror, but then she was knocked flat on her back and everything went dark.

15
Gumboots
Gets Squashed

Elspeth looked at Rory and put a finger to her lips. She was sure she could hear shouting in the distance.

"Did you hear that?" she whispered.

Rory shook his head.

Elspeth looked over to where Jack and Fern were putting their rucksacks on, ready to start moving again. They were deep in conversation and didn't seem to have noticed anything. But Elspeth felt uneasy.

"I can't see Uma Gumboots anywhere," she said quietly. "I don't want to scare the twins, but I think something's wrong."

"Not … Miss Crabb?" Rory asked, his eyes big.

"Maybe. We'd better find out," Elspeth said, making her way towards the creek.

"Elspeth, no, it's dangerous!" Rory hissed, but when he saw Elspeth was going to go anyway, he sighed and followed her.

The path down to the creek was overgrown and bright with wild flowers and strange plants. Elspeth felt more and more anxious as she walked. It was far too quiet – Uma Gumboots usually did everything at top volume. Elspeth paused at the water's edge, then her eyes widened.

There were two sets of footprints in the mud near the river. Fresh footprints, and not as large as Uma Gumboots' enormous ones.

"Crabb and Goulash have been here, I just know it," Elspeth whispered to Rory. She looked around carefully, then tiptoed towards the footprints. She scanned the area, looking for clues. And then she spotted a patch of bush that looked as if it had been squashed. One of Uma Gumboots' pans was lying upside down behind it. Elspeth moved closer, and as she parted the leaves she saw a shock of bright blond hair.

"Uma Gumboots!" Elspeth cried.

She shoved
her way
through the
undergrowth.

"Mmmmmf! Grrrppph! Gnnnnnh!" was all Uma Gumboots could say, because a smelly old sock was stuffed in her mouth. Her hands and feet were tightly tied as well.

Elspeth pulled the sock out of her mouth and Uma Gumboots spat on the ground.

"URGH," she said. "That woman nearly killed me, jumping on me from a tree!" Then she winced. "My head hurts."

Elspeth's mind was racing. "Crabb and Goulash have to be nearby," she whispered to Rory.

Rory held Lazlo up and he sniffed the air suspiciously, but then jumped back on to Rory's shoulder as normal.

"They must have gone," Rory said. "Lazlo would smell them otherwise."

Elspeth turned back to Uma Gumboots, wondering how to get her free. "Your Fix-It-Mate tool!" she said. "Where is it?"

"Top pocket," Uma Gumboots said weakly, and Elspeth grabbed it and flipped it open so it worked as a knife.

"Just hold still," she said. Uma Gumboots did as she was told. Elspeth hacked at the knots, and in a few minutes Uma Gumboots' hands and feet were free. But when she tried to walk, she was very wobbly.

"Think I took a hit to the head," she said, sounding much less bossy than usual.

"I'm seeing two of everything."

Elspeth and Rory helped Uma Gumboots move slowly back towards the camp, and Jack and Fern ran over to help.

"Two Ferns! Two Jacks!" mumbled Uma Gumboots, sitting down with a thud.

"Miss Crabb?" asked Jack grimly.

"Crabb and Goulash, I'd say," nodded Elspeth. "Someone jumped out of a tree and squashed Uma. I found her tied up in the bushes."

Fern helped Uma Gumboots to lie down. "I think Auntie Uma should stay here and rest," she said. "We can camp here tonight and head home tomorrow when she's feeling better."

Elspeth bit her lip. She couldn't stop now. Not with her parents still somewhere in the rainforest.

"I'm so sorry Miss Crabb hurt your auntie," she said. "But I've GOT to keep looking for Mum and Dad. I can't stop now. Besides, it's me that Crabb and Goulash are after, not you. You'll be safer without me!"

Jack and Fern looked at one another and frowned.

"But, Elspeth, you don't know the rainforest…" Fern started.

"… and it's not an easy place to trek through," Jack added.

Elspeth thought for a moment, but it only took a second for her to decide.

"I know it's dangerous," she said. "But I'm going on, as soon as it gets light again."

"If you're sure," Jack said, "it's about a day's trek to the waterfall from here. You'll reach it if you stay on this path. When the path forks, take the right fork, OK?"

The next morning Elspeth got up at sunrise. She felt hot and sticky after a night in the tent, but she only paused long enough to splash a little water on her face. She wanted to get going at once.

"Take some food with you," Fern said, coming out of her tent. She piled some fruit and energy bars into Elspeth's bag.

"And the Fix-It-Mate," Jack added. "Auntie Uma's still fast asleep, but she would want you to have it."

"Thank you," Elspeth said, tucking the Fix-It-Mate into her pocket. "I hope your auntie feels better soon." She lifted up her rucksack, trying to feel brave, but her knees were shaking a little bit. She had no idea what might be out there.

Then Elspeth heard a noise behind her. She turned round to see Rory putting on his rucksack, too.

"If you're going, I'm coming with you," Rory said in a determined voice, and Lazlo popped his head out of Rory's rucksack as if to agree.

Elspeth looked at Rory and smiled. Even when he was afraid, he still stuck with her. She squeezed his hand. "Thank you, Rory," she said quietly.

Jack and Fern hugged them goodbye, and Elspeth and Rory stepped back on to the trail, watching out for Miss Crabb and Gladys Goulash at every step.

16
Very Nasty
Things on the Trail

After squashing Uma Gumboots, tying her up with old tights and stuffing a sock in her mouth, Miss Crabb had dragged Gladys Goulash back on to the trail.

"Eee-hee-hee," she said. "That's got rid of the big blond woman. Now we've just got stupid little kids to deal with. Easy-peasy! We'll wait and see where they're going, then sneak ahead of them to dig our big pit."

"Yeah! And then Elspeth will fall right in it!" said Gladys Goulash.

"Indeed," Miss Crabb said. "You're finally getting the idea. About time, you blithering idiot."

Miss Crabb and Gladys Goulash clambered deep into the bushes next to the path. They smeared some moss and green sludge from the creek on their faces so they would be camouflaged, and then they spent a very hot and uncomfortable night sleeping on the carrier bags they had been using as waterproofs. And the next morning, Elspeth and Rory walked right past them.

But Elspeth had been keeping a close eye on the ground and she could see two sets of footprints on the path ahead of them. When the footprints stopped, Elspeth knew

Miss Crabb had stopped, too. She knew they must be hiding close by. But Elspeth walked on, pretending she hadn't noticed anything. It was a good few minutes before Elspeth dared whisper to Rory about what she'd seen.

"They're behind us," she said to Rory in a low voice when they stopped to drink from their water bottles. The heat was getting worse and it felt hard to breathe. "Crabb and Goulash's footprints stopped back there, so they must be behind us now." Elspeth's heart was pounding. It was horrible, knowing they were being followed.

"Elspeth," Rory paused, the water bottle lifted halfway to his lips. "I hear something."

Sure enough, Elspeth could hear it, too – the soft rustle of someone walking ahead of them along the path.

"It can't be Crabb and Goulash," Elspeth whispered. "Perhaps it's Mum and Dad! We need to get high up, then we might be able to see what's going on. Can you give me a leg up on to this tree?"

Rory held out his hands and Elspeth put her foot into them, then he pushed as hard as he could and Elspeth clambered up through thick leaves. She wriggled along a branch until she had a good view of the path. It was just as Jack had told her – there was a fork not far ahead. Then she gasped. Along the left-hand fork, on the other side of some big flat rocks, Bob and Belinda were setting up a tent.

"It's the couple who locked me in that horrible hut!" she said. "Bob and Belinda! They must have realized I've escaped, and they've come after me!"

Elspeth
jumped softly back
down to the path
and looked at Rory, who was
staring at her in horror. For a
second she was utterly at a loss.
How could she find her mum
and dad when
there was
danger in front of
her *and* behind
her?

Rory saw the fear in Elspeth's eyes. "Don't panic," he said quickly, grabbing her arms and facing her. "Elspeth, look at me. You'll think of something. You always do."

But with every second that passed, Elspeth worried that she wouldn't find her mum and dad in time. She looked at Rory and tried to think.

"Bob and Belinda don't know that Miss Crabb and Gladys Goulash are in the rainforest, too," Rory said quietly.

Elspeth stared at him and a tiny seed of a thought planted itself in her brain. "You're right," she said slowly. "And Crabb and Goulash can't know that Bob and Belinda are in the rainforest. So if we could lure Miss Crabb and Gladys Goulash towards Bob and Belinda…"

"They'd all bump into each other, buying

us time to escape!" said Rory, his eyes bright. "That's what we need to do, Elspeth!"

Elspeth pulled her notebook and pencil from her backpack. "I know," she said. "I'll leave a note stuck on a branch, pretending it's for you. I'll say that I'm setting up camp at the rocks, and that you must come and find me."

Rory started to smile. "Yes!" he said. "But when Miss Crabb goes there, she'll bump straight into Bob and Belinda!"

"We'll need a very good hiding place while all this goes on," Elspeth said. "We can't run the risk of anyone seeing us." She wiped the sweat off her forehead. "We'll climb up a tree again," she said. "Not this one – one a bit further towards Bob and Belinda. That way, we'll be able to see what happens more clearly."

Elspeth started writing. The pencil was slippery in her sweaty hand as she wrote.

Elspeth made the letters as big as possible, then she stuck the note on a sharp branch, so anyone coming along the path would see it at once.

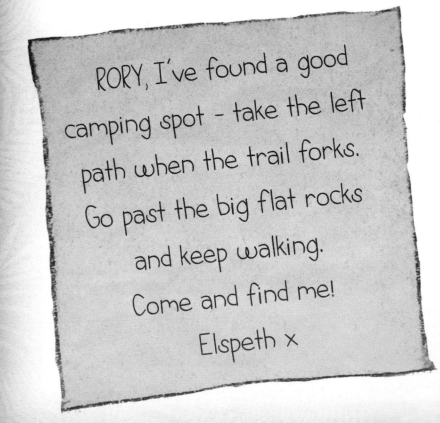

RORY, I've found a good camping spot – take the left path when the trail forks.
Go past the big flat rocks and keep walking.
Come and find me!
Elspeth x

"Hurry!" she said, grabbing Rory's hand, and they moved quietly along the trail for a few minutes and climbed up to their hiding place. They could just make out the path with Elspeth's note stuck on a tree, and then, if they craned their necks slightly, they could see Bob and Belinda's camp. If their plan didn't work, they were stuck in the most dangerous place possible.

"Don't make a sound," Elspeth mouthed to Rory.

17
The Fork in the Trail

Bob and Belinda were setting up camp and having a big row about whose job it was to dig a toilet trench.

"You do it! It was your idea to come into this stupid rainforest!" shrieked Belinda, giving Bob a shove.

"All right, all right," mumbled Bob moodily. He moved to the edge of their camping spot and started digging a long, shallow trench.

"For goodness' sake, I could do much better than that!" hissed Belinda, peering down at the trench. Then they heard heavy footsteps coming towards them.

"It's Elspeth Hart's parents! Must be!" said Bob, his eyes lighting up. He threw down his shovel. "Let's grab them and claim our reward!"

Bob stepped out smartly from behind the flat rocks. Then he gave a yell of horror, because instead of Elspeth's parents, he came eyeball to eyeball with two very sweaty, dirty women.

"EEEH!" shrieked Miss Crabb. "Who are you?"

"Who are we? Who are YOU, more like?" shouted Belinda, who was in a filthy mood anyway and quite happy to get into a fight. "Aren't you the meat pie women? What are you doing, creeping around the rainforest?"

"Gah!" Miss Crabb swatted at Belinda with her sun hat, and Belinda gave her a hard shove. Miss Crabb flared her nostrils. Then she launched herself at Belinda and they wrestled furiously.

"Fight! Brilliant!" shouted Gladys, leaping on Bob and knocking him over.

It was a very muddy, dirty fight, with flip-flops being used as weapons and plenty of nasty kicking and biting. Bob and Belinda were mean and ruthless, but soon it was obvious that Miss Crabb and Gladys Goulash were going to win.

Elspeth and Rory didn't wait around to see what happened. "Quick, there's no time to lose," Elspeth said. "We have to take the path to the right while they're distracted." They slithered down the tree and crept away.

Behind them, Miss Crabb gave a crow of victory as she trussed Belinda and Bob up with bits of old knicker elastic, and rolled them both into their own toilet trench.

The path on the right was overgrown, although Elspeth could make out a faint trail to follow. Had her parents come this way? Elspeth couldn't be sure. She hadn't seen any sweet wrappers for ages.

"We should start leaving our own markers, just in case," Elspeth said to Rory. "We don't want to get lost and not be able to find our way back." She dug around in her rucksack and found her notebook, then tore a strip off one of the pages.

Then she took the scrap of white paper and snagged it on a branch. She was careful to put it low down, where a grown-up wouldn't spot it.

They kept going, pausing to leave a marker every few minutes. The journey was sweaty and difficult. After a few hours,

Elspeth paused to catch her breath, and heard the sound of running water.

"Do you hear that?" Elspeth asked Rory. "It's louder than the rivers we've passed. Do you think it could be the waterfall?"

They pushed their way towards the sound, and when Elspeth had hacked her way through another overgrown patch of leaves, they clambered through and stopped in astonishment. They were next to a deep green pool. As they looked up … and up … and up … all they could see was a huge stream of water pouring down.

"The waterfall! We made it!" Rory said in awe, grabbing Lazlo as he tried to run towards the pool. He had to shout to make himself heard over the noise of the thundering water. It was like three hundred showers had all been switched on at once.

They both stepped back so they wouldn't get splashed.

"But what now…?" Elspeth murmured, scanning the route ahead of them. She could understand why Fern and Jack had warned her not to go any further.

The trail wound around the side of the pool and then disappeared into dense trees. The rainforest seemed much darker and thicker here, and Elspeth could tell it would be very easy to get lost.

"I haven't seen a sweet wrapper for a while," Elspeth continued. "Maybe Mum and Dad didn't come this way…"

She stepped carefully around the edge of the pool, but there were no clues to be found. Elspeth felt like the rainforest was closing in on her. Miss Crabb and Gladys Goulash were somewhere back down the trail with Bob and Belinda, and it wouldn't be long before they came after her.

"You know what's up there, if we keep following that path," Rory said. He swallowed nervously.

"I know," Elspeth said. "The Lost Valley." She looked at Rory, her heart beating fast. "But we must keep going. We might find another clue. And if we go back, Miss Crabb will catch us."

18
Beyond the Waterfall

Elspeth and Rory followed the narrow
trail up through the trees. Once or twice,
the path seemed to disappear completely.
Elspeth couldn't be sure they were going
the right way, but anything was better than
staying in one place and waiting for Miss
Crabb to pounce. As they went, she left
little white markers for the way back.

Rory was out of breath. He stopped by the side of the path and took a swig of water. His cheeks were even pinker than usual.

"I don't know about this, Elspeth," he said. "It's getting dark."

Elspeth looked up at the sky and frowned. Rory was right – the light was starting to go. "We'd better stop for the night," she said. She wriggled out of her rucksack and found a clear spot with enough space for their tent. The ground sloped steeply, but it would have to do.

Rory got the tent out of his rucksack and they put it up – they'd learned how to do it by watching Jack and Fern. The sky grew dark above them while they munched on a squashed banana and some dry biscuits.

But when it was time to go to sleep, Elspeth lay wide awake, listening out for

every little crack and animal call outside.
Miss Crabb must have stopped for the night
as well, surely? And Bob and Belinda?
Or were they all creeping through the
undergrowth, getting closer? *No*, she told
herself. *Don't be silly.*

Elspeth turned over, wriggling right
down in her sleeping bag. She couldn't help
thinking of Jack's story about kangaroos that
attacked people. And crocodiles… But they
wouldn't stray so far from water, would they?
Finally she closed her eyes, but she dreamed
of a strange howling sound all night.

"Elspeth! It's light! Let's get going!"

Elspeth woke with a jolt. Rory was
shaking her arm to wake her. She rubbed
her eyes and looked through the open flap

of the tent. It was bright and sunny and the heat was blasting down on them again.

Rory smiled at Elspeth, but he had dark shadows under his eyes. Even Lazlo looked a bit tired. He was running around more slowly than usual.

"Thanks, Rory," Elspeth said, taking the cup of water he held out. "I couldn't sleep for ages, but I guess I must have drifted off at some point. What about you?"

"Hardly slept at all," Rory said, rolling up his sleeping bag. "I kept wondering if Miss Crabb was going to jump out at us. Or that horrible couple who kidnapped you." He looked at Elspeth. "Are you OK?"

"I think so," Elspeth said, splashing a bit of water on her face. "Let's keep moving."

They packed everything up as quickly as they could and ploughed on through the rainforest. After about an hour, Elspeth thought she could see a path veering off to her right, so she marked a tree with a scrap of paper and pushed her way through the branches. Suddenly she burst out of the dark trees and found herself on a wobbly ledge, with nothing in front of her but sky.

"WOAH!" Elspeth yelled, teetering forward. She spun her arms wildly, trying to get her balance. Beneath her was a vast canyon of red earth, hundreds of metres deep. Terrified, Elspeth grabbed behind her. Her fingers slipped off leaves and she scrabbled harder, desperate to get hold of something. She managed to find a branch and Rory grasped her dress, pulling her back to safety. One more step and she would have fallen into the huge bowl of the valley below.

"Elspeth! I thought you were going to go over the edge…" Rory was shaking and still clinging to Elspeth's dress.

Elspeth sat down on a rock, her legs unsteady. "This must be it," she said. "The Lost Valley."

They stared in silence for a few minutes, taking it all in. The Lost Valley was like a big empty basin, with the bottom far, far below them. There was nothing down there but scrubby plants and rocks, and all around the edge, where they were standing, were overgrown trees.

"We have to go back the way we came," Rory said. "This place is dangerous. Elspeth? Are you listening to me?"

Elspeth was staring across the valley with wide eyes. "Rory," she said without turning to look at him, "pass me the binoculars."

Elspeth put the binoculars to her eyes, adjusting them so the far side of the valley came into sharp focus. Then she took a sharp breath as she spotted two tiny shapes.

It was her mum and dad.

19
Elspeth's Mum and Dad

"MUM! DAD!" Elspeth screamed at the top of her voice. She turned to Rory. "It's them, it's actually them!"

Elspeth and Rory yelled until their throats hurt, but it was no use. Her mum and dad were too far away to hear. Elspeth realized there were tears running down her face.

"They're alive, Rory, they're alive!" she said, and she sat down on the rock, feeling like her legs couldn't hold her any longer.

Rory put his arm around her shoulder and Lazlo hopped on to her knee, trying to help.

Elspeth looked through the binoculars again. Her parents were sipping water from a bottle. They both looked very tired.

"Look," Rory said, "there's a tiny track. That's how they must have got through the valley."

Elspeth looked down, and saw the track. But the valley was so deep that it would take ages to get all the way to the bottom and then up again the other side.

"There's got to be another route," she said. "We need to catch up with them quickly, before they start moving again."

Elspeth looked left and right. The rainforest was so thick that it was like a green wall all around the rim of the valley. But then she spotted a very narrow ledge. They'd have to go carefully, but Elspeth was sure they could do it.

"We're not going to go down into the valley," Elspeth said. "We're going to go *around* it." She tore off another white marker and stuck it on a branch, then she stepped down on to the ledge and started moving slowly and carefully along it.

"Elspeth, it's very narrow," Rory said nervously, "and Lazlo's not good with heights."

Elspeth stretched out her hand to him. "Come on, Rory, you can do it!" she said. "We're so close. We can't give up now."

Rory followed her on to the ledge and

Elspeth smiled to reassure him, but when she started moving, she had to tell herself not to look down. She inched her way forward, clinging to the side of the rock, taking her time. Sometimes the trail in front of her looked fragile, and she tested the path with her toe before stepping forward. Once she kicked a small rock off the edge and it clattered down the side of the valley, but it was so deep she didn't even hear it land on the bottom.

When they were about halfway along, Elspeth heard a sinister noise … a kind of whistling sound. She froze, hanging on to the rock next to her.

Whooooo … hoo-whoooo…

"What was that?" Rory asked in a wobbly voice.

As they stood there, not daring to move, the sound got louder, until it sounded like somebody crying. A knot of fear tightened in Elspeth's stomach. She held on to the rock and looked down into the valley, then around the edge, but she couldn't see anything. No animals. No people. The wind ruffled her hair and shook the trees beside them. And still the sound got louder.

Elspeth turned and caught Rory's eye. She'd never seen him look so afraid.

"The stories are true," he whispered.

"The valley is haunted. Elspeth, what are we going to do?"

Lazlo was scared, too. He leaped off Rory's shoulder and scrabbled his way up the rock next to them. Then he vanished into a hole.

"Lazlo, come back here!" Rory cried, reaching out to grab him.

Elspeth looked up as Rory coaxed Lazlo out. There wasn't just one hole in the rock, she realized. There were lots and lots, dotted around the sides of the valley. And as she looked around at them, the wind died down – and the howling noise stopped.

"It's not ghosts! It's the wind!" Elspeth cried. "Rory, do you see all those little holes in the rock, like the one Lazlo went into? The wind is whistling through them, that's what's making the spooky noise!"

They paused for a minute until the wind whipped up again and sure enough, the low whistling started, building up to sound like a howl.

"Well done, Lazlo!" Elspeth said. "You've solved the mystery of the Lost Valley!" She turned back to Rory, her face determined. "There are no ghosts! We can keep moving towards Mum and Dad!"

20
The Edge
of the Lost Valley

After fighting with Bob and Belinda, tying them up and leaving them in their own toilet trench, Miss Crabb and Gladys Goulash finally arrived at the edge of the Lost Valley.

Miss Crabb spotted the gap in the trees and shoved Gladys through. Gladys gave a screech as she stepped out into nothingness, then Miss Crabb pulled her back to safety.

"Gah!" said Miss Crabb. "Which way did the little rat go?" She peered though her binoculars and saw Elspeth's parents on the far side of the valley. "Aha! There are the stupid parents. But where's Elspeth and that Snitter boy?"

"I dunno," said Gladys Goulash. "But I'm *hungry!*"

Miss Crabb reached over and slapped Gladys Goulash on the head without even bothering to look at her. Then she scanned the valley and spotted Elspeth and Rory making their way around the edge.

"Sneaky little toad," Miss Crabb said. "She's found a shortcut. But we're going to start digging our pit, Gladys Goulash. They'll have to come back this way eventually. And we'll be ready for them."

Elspeth and Rory were almost at the other side of the valley, but it had felt like the longest, slowest journey of Elspeth's life. She kept reaching out a toe to check the ledge was steady, then stepping forward, then pausing again. But finally Elspeth helped Rory clamber off the ledge. She gripped his hand tightly as they made their way to where she had seen her mum and dad.

And then she was running, as fast as she could. Her parents looked up in astonishment and Elspeth threw her arms around both of them at once.

"It's … it's … it's Elspeth!" her dad stammered in amazement. "It's really you!" He tilted Elspeth's chin up so he could look into her eyes, and then he grabbed her into a hug again. "Our little girl!"

Elspeth's mum just held on to her daughter with tears rolling down her face.

"How did you get here? Are you all right? Who took you?" her dad asked. And then he looked up and spotted Rory, standing shyly to one side, holding Lazlo. "And who is this?"

Elspeth and Rory sat down with her mum and dad and told them the whole story. Her parents interrupted with questions now and again as Elspeth told them about being kidnapped by Miss Crabb, and about following Miss Crabb on to a cruise ship all the way to America, and about Mr Tunnock flying them to Australia, and about Uma Gumboots and Jack and Fern and Bob and Belinda.

"Where have you been for the last year?" Elspeth asked, looking up first at her dad, and then at her mum. "Someone told you to look for me in Australia, didn't they?"

"Oh, Elspeth, we've been searching all over the world," her mum said, and her eyes filled up with tears again. "But a couple of weeks ago we got a phone call saying you might be in the Never-ending Rainforest, so we flew out here at once. We came as far as we could by train and then hitchhiked to Starry Bay. We've been leaving posters everywhere and asking if anyone had seen you. We were just desperate…" Elspeth's mum sobbed and Elspeth gave her another big hug.

"The storm last week was pretty ferocious," Elspeth's dad said. He pushed his glasses further up on his nose. "We dug ourselves in and just had to wait it out. A lot of our stuff got washed away though … including our phone and our food. Then we thought we'd go further into the rainforest, but we got lost."

"It was only yesterday that we found our way back to this valley," Elspeth's mum added. "We were going to start trekking back to Starry Bay today. We haven't eaten for days."

Rory scrabbled in Elspeth's rucksack and brought out some energy bars.

"You can eat these!" he said, handing them to Elspeth's parents.

Elspeth went on with their story. "Our new friends Jack and Fern have gone back to Crocodile Creek with Uma Gumboots," she explained. "But Miss Crabb and Gladys Goulash are in the rainforest somewhere, looking for me. AND the couple who tried to kidnap me to get the reward money … they're here, too!"

"What?" Elspeth's dad said. "They're all in the rainforest, after my little girl?" His face crinkled into an angry frown. "Don't worry. We're with you now, and Miss Crabb can't hurt you any more."

Elspeth's mum stroked her hair reassuringly, but Elspeth saw the worried expression on her face.

"We'd better head towards civilization," her mum said. "Can we go back the way you came, sweetheart?"

Elspeth nodded, but she scanned the valley anxiously as they got ready to go. With Miss Crabb around, nobody was ever really safe.

They retraced the route along the ledge, with Elspeth's dad going first this time.

He moved even more slowly and
carefully than Elspeth had done, pausing
every so often to make sure everyone behind
him was OK.

Soon the wind started whistling through
the rocks.

"We've heard that strange noise a
few times," Elspeth's dad said. He stared

around the valley, frowning.

"It's OK, Dad! It's the little holes in the rocks!" Elspeth held on tight to the rock on her left and carefully pointed up with her right hand. "They make a scary sound when the wind goes through them!"

"Really?" Elspeth's dad looked up at the holes in the rock, then gave her a proud smile. "Aren't you clever for working it out? On we go, then." He stepped forward carefully. *Test-step-pause. Test-step-pause.* Elspeth felt like they were moving in slow motion. She kept looking across the valley for Miss Crabb, feeling very uneasy.

But finally Elspeth's dad stepped back on to solid ground and turned around to help everyone off the little ledge.

"Elspeth Hart, I can't believe you came around that ledge!" Elspeth's mum scolded her suddenly, then gave her a tight hug. "It was so dangerous!"

"But I had to, Mum!" Elspeth said. "I would have done anything to find you! Come on, we need to follow my little white markers back."

"Yes, it should be simple from now on," Rory said hopefully. "Lazlo's desperate to get back, look!"

Lazlo had jumped down from Rory's shoulder. He sniffed the ground and turned to look at Rory, acting very strangely.

"What's wrong, Lazlo?" Rory asked, stepping forward to pick him up.

Elspeth grabbed Rory's arm and stopped. She turned to her mum and dad and put a finger to her lips. Lazlo had just helped her to notice something very suspicious.

21
The Strange Thing About the Path

There was something strange about a large section of path in front of them, just where Lazlo had stopped to sniff the ground.

Elspeth stared at it very closely. "Something's wrong," she said at once. "Don't take another step forward."

Elspeth tried to puzzle out what was bothering her. Then she realized. There were lots of big leaves and twigs on the ground, many more than on the rest of the trail. "Someone's been here," she whispered. "This looks like a trap." She picked up the biggest rock she could see, and hurled it ahead of her on to the path.

The stone landed on the leaves and vanished. There was a pause before they heard a thud below.

"I knew it," said Elspeth. "It's a trap! Crabb and Goulash must have dug a pit here, expecting us to fall into it!"

"Well spotted, Elspeth," said her dad. "So they won't be far away?" he added in a low voice.

"Oh, they're around here somewhere, I know it," Elspeth said angrily. She stared round at the trees. "If you're watching this, Miss Crabb, you haven't won! We found your stupid trap! Where are you? Come out, if you think you're so brave!"

There was a rustling sound and Miss Crabb appeared from behind a bush, her face smeared with dirt. Then there was the sound of snapping twigs and Gladys Goulash appeared behind Miss Crabb, peering round her and licking her lips.

"We've finally got you all together," said Miss Crabb, sounding very pleased with herself. "What a shame you spotted my trap. But isn't it lucky that I brought something else with me? A huge, indestructible WHALE-CATCHING NET!" And with that, she stepped forward and threw the enormous net over all of them.

Elspeth leaped to one side, but Rory and her parents weren't quick enough. The net landed on top of them with a *whoosh*.

"NO! Elspeth!" her mum cried out in terror.

Elspeth threw herself forward, trying to get them free, but it was no use.

Miss Crabb shoved Elspeth so hard that she flew up in the air and landed on the ground with a thump. Then Gladys Goulash plonked herself on the edge of the net, so they couldn't get out from under it. Elspeth could see her dad tearing at the net, but there was no way it was going to break.

Now Miss Crabb was moving closer to her with a cruel look in her eyes. "Oh dear," she said. "Poor little Elspeth is all alone again. All I need to do is throw her in my pit of spiders until she gives me that precious recipe."

She stepped towards Elspeth and Elspeth did the only thing she could think of. She ran.

Elspeth raced away through the rainforest. She ducked and weaved and leaped over twisty branches and slippery boulders, and she ran left then right then left again. She could hear Miss Crabb behind her, gasping for breath. Gladys Goulash was behind Miss Crabb – Elspeth could tell from the clumpy footsteps. Elspeth knew she was faster than Gladys Goulash, but she wasn't sure if she could outrun Miss Crabb. Miss Crabb was very determined. Elspeth knew she wouldn't be giving up any time soon.

Elspeth twisted and turned until she was certain she was moving back towards the path. She jumped over a fallen log, and then she slowed down, just a little bit. Miss Crabb and Gladys Goulash were right behind her now.

"Ha!" Elspeth could hear Miss Crabb muttering between wheezy breaths. "You can't run forever, you little slugface!"

Elspeth kept running. She ducked and swerved around trees, going in a big circle, until she could see the leaves scattered over the path. She was back at the big pit. Elspeth tried to calculate how big that pit was. Could she jump it? Would she make it to the other side?

Elspeth felt Miss Crabb's claw-like hands graze her back. It was now or never.

Elspeth jumped.

22
The Biggest Jump Ever

Elspeth held her breath and flung herself forward. *Please, please, please,* she thought, *let me get to the other side!*

The tip of her trainer touched earth and then Elspeth hit the ground face down, scrabbling to pull her other foot up out of the pit. She dragged herself up and turned around, just in time to see Miss Crabb and Gladys Goulash race on to the leaves towards her … and drop into the depths of the big dark pit.

"AAAARGH!" shrieked Miss Crabb as she fell.

"OOOOOOOFFFF!" groaned Gladys Goulash as she fell.

There were two thuds, one louder than the other, and then silence. Elspeth stood up and peered over the edge.

She could see Miss Crabb and Gladys Goulash at the bottom of a very dark and muddy pit, looking a bit stunned. They sat up and then there was a loud screech.

"There's spiders flippin' everywhere!" Miss Crabb was shouting. "This is all your fault, Gladys Goulash!"

"No, it's not!" Gladys Goulash shouted back. "You're the one who thought we should set a trap. Ooh! Ouch! There's a spider down my vest!"

"EEEEH! Ow! There's a spider in my knickers!" shouted Miss Crabb. "Ooh, I feel sick!"

Elspeth hurried over to her mum and dad and Rory.

"Elspeth! That was so brave!" cried Rory. "Can you get us out of here?"

Elspeth grabbed Uma Gumboots' Fix-It-Mate, flicked it open, and cut them free.

Then she realized she could hear a very welcome sound indeed.

It was the sound of Uma Gumboots shouting in the distance. "No mucking about, no leaving the trail and no dropping litter!" she was saying. Elspeth ran forward and saw Uma Gumboots, Jack and Fern coming towards them.

"Here!" she shouted, waving her arms in the air. "Over here!"

"Auntie Uma refused to go back to Crocodile Creek when she came round," Fern said, hurrying towards Elspeth.

"She was so angry about being squashed…"

"…she insisted we come and find you as fast as we could!" Jack said. "Elspeth, are you OK?"

Before Elspeth could answer, Uma Gumboots caught up with them.

"I want to see those nasty ladies get their comeuppance!" Uma Gumboots shouted. "And we found Bob and Belinda, those kidnapping good-for-nothings! Did you tie 'em up and chuck 'em in that toilet trench?"

"No! Miss Crabb did that!" Elspeth said.

"Ha! Well, just you wait until I have a word with them. Those greedy galahs!" said Uma Gumboots. She stopped short as she caught sight of Elspeth's mum and dad.

"Stone the crows! You found your oldies!" she shouted happily.

"Mum, Dad, this is Uma Gumboots and Jack and Fern," Elspeth said in a rush. "They've been ever so helpful and kind. Uma Gumboots, we've caught Miss Crabb and Gladys Goulash in their own trap!"

Uma Gumboots gave Elspeth's parents a bone-crushing handshake, and then they all stood around the pit looking down at Miss Crabb and Gladys Goulash. They were both shrieking at the top of their voices and hopping around trying to get the spiders out of their clothes. Every so often one of them would try to slither up the side of the muddy pit, but it was far too steep for them to escape.

"I suppose," Elspeth's dad said, "we'll need to get back to the nearest town and phone the police."

Elspeth and Rory looked at each other.

"Crabb and Goulash escaped from prison before. They could escape again," Elspeth said.

Uma Gumboots scratched her head. "I've got it!" she said. "I need someone to look after the koalas – make sure they've got enough food and clean up their poo once Jack and Fern go home. I could use those ladies in Crocodile Creek. They won't be going anywhere else, trust me!" And she gave a big guffaw of laughter.

"That's perfect! Miss Crabb is TERRIFIED of koalas! One of the pupils at the School for Show-offs had a fluffy toy koala and Miss Crabb screamed when she saw it!" Elspeth gasped. "What do you think, Miss Crabb? Fancy a job as a koala-keeper?"

"NOOOOO!" Miss Crabb let out a blood-curdling scream. "Not koalas! Anything but koalas! Not something CUTE and FLUFFY like koalas!" She curled herself into a ball and started shaking with terror.

Gladys Goulash let out a frightened burp and started talking gibberish. The Bitey Bitey spider poison was turning both their faces a horrid green colour.

"I think you and the koalas will live happily ever after," said Elspeth.

"Come on, let's get back to town," said Uma Gumboots. "I'll come back and collect these two later, when I get Bob and Belinda. Ha! We can fix up Crocodile Creek and get some paying guests again! I'll be able to set up my koala hospital at last! I also thought Mr T might like to stay on and help me. I'm kinda fond of him. Good bloke."

Elspeth caught Rory's eye and tried not to laugh at the thought of Mr Tunnock staying with Uma Gumboots. Then she thought about the bouncy kangaroos and the sweet koalas, and was very glad Uma Gumboots would be able to keep Crocodile Creek open.

"What happened in the Lost Valley?" Fern asked eagerly. "Did you hear awful howling noises? Did you see any ghosts?"

"There aren't any ghosts!" Elspeth said. "The creepy noises were just the wind whistling through holes in the rocks! Lazlo helped us work it out."

She grinned at Rory, Jack and Fern. Then she took hold of her mum and dad's hands. She couldn't believe she had her parents back at last.

And then Uma Gumboots led the way, and Jack, Fern and Rory started walking through the Never-ending Rainforest, followed by Elspeth and her mum and dad.

It was finally time to go home.

Read how it all began...

Sarah Forbes

Elspeth Hart
and the
School for Show-offs

OUT NOW!

Sarah Forbes

Elspeth Hart
and the
Perlious Voyage

Sarah
Forbes

Sarah was born in Aberdeen and currently lives in Edinburgh. She used to work on magazines, interviewing pop stars for a living, but now she works as an editor, helping other writers. Sarah loves dreaming up new adventures for Elspeth Hart.

James Brown filled in an important careers questionnaire when he was thirteen and it told him he was definitely going to be a teacher and an illustrator. It was right! James lives in Nottingham and draws in front of a mirror.

James
Brown